AF673506

TIBETAN TALES

STORIES FROM THE DSANGS BLUN

(The Wise and The Foolish)

TIBETAN TALES

STORIES FROM THE DSANGS BLUN
(The Wise and The Foolish)

From an ancient collection of stories on the wise and foolish actions of men, attributed to the Buddha Gautama and compiled after his death by his disciple, Ananda.

Translated from the Tibetan
by
Antoinette K. Gordon

PILGRIMS

PILGRIMS PUBLISHING
◆ Varanasi ◆

Tibetan Tales Stories from the Dsangs Blun
Ethel Beswick

Published by:
PILGRIMS PUBLISHING

An imprint of:
PILGRIMS BOOK HOUSE
(Distributors in India)
B 27/98 A-8, Nawabganj Road
Durga Kund, Varanasi-221010, India
Tel: 91-542-2314060,
Fax: 91-542-2312456
E-mail: pilgrims@satyam.net.in
Website: www.pilgrimsbooks.com

Copyright © 2007, Pilgrims Publishing
All Rights Reserved

ISBN: 81-7769-503-7

The contents of this book may not be reproduced, stored or copied in any form—printed, electronic, photocopied, or otherwise—except for excerpts used in review, without the written permission of the publisher.

Printed in India at Pilgrim Press Pvt. Ltd. Lalpur Varanasi

This book is dedicated to
WILLIAM JOHN GORDON
by his devoted grandmother
in the hope that some day
he will enjoy reading these
stories as much as she has
enjoyed translating them.

ACKNOWLEDGMENTS

I wish to acknowledge my gratitude to Professor Bernhard Geiger, of Columbia University, for his invaluable help with the intricacies of Tibetan grammar; to Peter Fingesten, Pace College, for reading the manuscript and making valuable suggestions, and to Chang Chen Chi, late of Nanking University, China, whose understanding of the religion and the Tibetan people was a great aid in interpreting some of the more obscure aspects of the tales.

A.K.G.

PREFACE

During the last decades there has been a great increase of interest in the ways, religion and folklore of the peoples of the East. This interest for the most part has resulted in scholarly treatises and economic research. Real progress will result only when we go to the thoughts and aspirations of the people themselves. We will realize then that basically the ideas and hopes are the same everywhere.

Tibetans live in a climate and under conditions very different from Occidentals. They follow a state religion, Lamaism, a form of Buddhism, which influences every phase of their daily lives. Therefore, the literature that has come out of Tibet is largely based on their religion. Buddhism was introduced into Tibet in the seventh century of our era and replaced to a great extent the indigenous and primitive Bön. Tibet is a complete theocracy, ruled by the Dalai Lama who is the temporal and spiritual ruler. The religious, monks and other attaches of the monasteries comprise almost thirty per cent. of the population. From this fact we may see how closely the life of the common people is interwoven with those who follow the monastic life.

In my studies I have learned much from these stories, and I would like to share with others the delight I had in reading the originals. They are taken from the "Dsangs-blun", a group of stories from the Kanjur which is a part of the canonical Buddhist writings. They are traditional stories which the Buddha Gautama (approximately 620 B.C.—543 B.C.) told to his disciples, and are in the form of parables which impart important aspects of the Doctrine. These stories have much in common with the ethics of many religions and by illustrating common incidents of life, point a moral. Such stories were as important to spread the basic tenets of the Buddhist Doctrine as were the more formal laws.

The Tibetan vocabulary is extremely rich. The various honorific forms of greeting and of speaking are difficult, sometimes almost impossible to translate. There are so many ways of expressing an idea, depending entirely on the person to whom one is speaking or from whom one is making a request. For example, when speaking to the Buddha, it is always phrased: "Ananda submitted this question (or request) to the Victoriously Consummated One." To a person of equal rank, the words "asked" or "said" would be used. And so with many other phrases.

In the Tibetan titles and words throughout the text, the diacritical marks have been omitted as being confusing to the layman. There is no standardized transliteration of Tibetan, so we have used approximate phonetic spellings. Sir Charles Bell, author of several Tibetan dictionaries and an able scholar of Tibetan, who lived in and near Tibet for 18 years had this to say about the problem of translations: "Tibetan is so highly condensed that it can hardly be translated into English within similar limits." In translating these stories, the Tibetan text has been followed as closely as possible in order to preserve the

Tibetan " flavour ". There were instances, however, where the literal translations would have been very awkward in English and had to be modified.

The explanations of certain technical terms and concepts have been placed at the end of each story, in order not to overburden the text with footnotes.

It is the hope of this translator that these stories will lead to greater interest and a better understanding not only of Tibetan Buddhism but of the Tibetan people as well.

A.K.G.

CONTENTS

This quotation is from the Tanjur, Section *mDo*, Vol. 21, leaf 27.

འཇིག་རྟེན་བདེ་བ་ཇི་སྙེད་པ་

ajig . rten . bde . ba . ji . sñed . pa

world (in) happiness whatever is

དེ་ཀུན་གཞན་བདེ་འདོད་ལས་བྱུང་

de . kun . gz'an . bde . 'dod . las . byuṅ

(of) all others happiness desire from arises

འཇིག་རྟེན་སྡུག་བསྔལ་ཇི་སྙེད་པ་

ajig . rten . sdug . bsṅal . ji . sñed . pa

world (in) misery whatever is

དེ་ཀུན་བདག་བདེ་འདོད་ལས་བྱུང་

de . kun . bdag . bde . 'dod . las . byun

(of) all self happiness desire from arises

Whatever happiness is in the world, it has arisen from a wish for the welfare of others.

Whatever misery is in the world, it has arisen from a wish for our own welfare.

Questions of The Deity of the Ocean

At one time these words were heard by me.

"THE VICTORIOUSLY CONSUMMATED ONE" was dwelling at Nanyod in the grove of Prince Rgyal Byed in the dwelling of a householder called Mgon med zas sbyin. At this time in this country about five hundred merchants who were going to sea to gather jewels, discussed this. "With us, among the men, there should be one, a wise one, a knowing one, to command as sea-captain." Having discussed this they took along a religious novice, and set out to the ocean. Arriving at the middle of the ocean, the deity of the ocean, transforming himself into a demon with a very ugly body, bluish-black, and fangs projecting upward, and a halo of flames burning about his head, came to the side of the ship, and said, " Deliver this ship to me ! "

Then to the merchants, he said these words, " Where in the world are there beings surpassing me in fearfulness ? " The novice answered, " There are many beings more terrifying than you are." The deity of the ocean said, " Who are they ? " The novice answered, " In the world, these are the fools and ignorant, who sin without fear or restraint, who cut off life and who take what has not been given, who commit unchastity and adultery, speak falsehoods and abusive words, speak words of calumny and slander, are lustful and prone to anger, and have bad views. These, changing life, are born as beings of hell. They are led by the guardians of the hell-beings to suffer many kinds of miseries , some indeed being cut to pieces by sharp instruments ; some indeed are cut into bits being dragged hither and thither by a wagon; some are attached to a mill; some mount on a hill of swords; some are boiled inside a wagon of fire; or in a boiling kettle and in ice; and in bad vomits, etc. These, suffering for a hundred thousand years, many kinds of infinite miseries, these indeed, are fit to be considered much more fearful than you are."

Thus he spoke, and the deity of the ocean, hearing, suddenly became invisible. Then afterwards they went further. The deity of the ocean, transforming himself into a man extremely emaciated and exhausted, nothing but skin and bones, said these words to the captain of the ship, "Deliver this ship to me." Then he asked, "Is there anyone in the world more emaciated and exhausted than me?" The novice answered, "There are greatly more exhausted and emaciated ones than you are." The deity of the ocean asked, "Who are they?" By the novice it was said, "The fools and ignorant ones who are selfish and avaricious; who are lustful and envious, not giving alms; these, dying, are born as tortured pirits with bodies like mountains, necks like needles, hair dishevelled, black and emaciated, not even hearing the name of water for a hundred thousand years, these indeed are much more emaciated even than you are." Thus he spoke and suddenly the deity became invisible.

Thereafter the ship went further along on the ocean. The deity transformed himself into a being of great beauty of face and form. "Deliver this ship to me," he said and to the merchants he said, "Among the world of man, is there one like me, as handsome in face and form?" The novice answered, "There are men a hundred times more beautiful than you." The deity of the ocean said, "Who are they who are more beautiful than I am?" The novice said, "In the world, the wise and good men, who, practising the ten virtues, being pure entirely in body, speech and mind; believing greatly in the three most precious ones; making offerings of their wealth; these intelligent beings, when dying, are born into the heavenly region, with face and form very beautiful and handsome. These indeed are a hundred thousand times more beautiful than you. When comparing you with these, it is like comparing a blind monkey with a goddess of beauty."

Then the deity of the ocean scooped up a handful of water, and asked the novice, " What is more, a handful of water or the water of the ocean ? " By the novice it was said, " While a handful of water is not much, the water of the ocean is indeed much less." The deity of the ocean said, " These words spoken by you, are they truth ? " The novice said, " These words are true, they are not falsehood." " How is it evident that they are true ? " " Undoubtedly a time of dryness will come, when the end of the kalpa approaches destruction. When two suns arise, the springs and ponds all dry up. When three suns arise, all the brooks will dry up. When four suns arise, all the rivers will dry up. When five suns arise, the great ocean will be diminished from its former size. When seven suns arise, the great ocean also will dry up. Mount Sumeru also will become destroyed by being ignited and burning to the border of jewels, but whoever by thoughts of complete faith, offers as much as a handful of water to the Buddha or to the priesthood, or to parents, or bestows on the poor, or offers to a beast to drink, these meritorious acts in many kalpas, are not consumed. For this reason the water of the ocean is little while the handful of water is indeed much more." Thereafter the deity of the ocean was very glad and to the novice he gave many jewels.

He also sent excellent jewels to Buddha and the priesthood. The novice and the merchants, having sufficient jewels, again returned happily to their country. And then the novice and the 500 merchants came to the place where the Buddha was. They made obeisance at the feet of the Buddha. Each one having brought jewels given by the Deity of the Ocean to Buddha and the priesthood, they kneeled and with hands clasped in devotion to the Victoriously Consummated One they submitted this request, "We wish to be taught the doctrine, in order to become monks," and the word was given by the Buddha, "Monks you are welcome." Hair and beard fell off by themselves, and they became monks clad in garments of the doctrine.

All the doctrine having been taught to them by the Buddha, all desire having been consumed, they became Arhants. The numerous retinue, by the explanations of the Buddha, were manifestly rejoicing and happy.

NOTES

Victoriously Consummated One—An epithet of the Buddha. Tibetan: *bcom ldan 'das*: The Victoriously Consummated One, because he has won perfection after a long and continuous struggle with worldly desires.

Mgon med zas sbyin—Name of the householder who made food offerings to Buddha and the priesthood.

Novice—A layman who has taken the 5 vows (i.e. not to kill; not to lie; not to slander; not to take what is not given; not to commit adultery)—but lives a secular life.

Beings of hell—In the cycle of rebirth or transmigration, there are 6 regions of rebirth. After the soul is judged, the deceased may be reborn into: (1) the region of the Gods; (2) the demi-gods; (3) the World of Man; (4) the Animal World; (5) the World of the Tortured Spirits called Pretas; or (6) Hell.

There are 8 hot hells and 8 cold hells and the punishments in these various hells, fit the sins and crimes of the individuals. Tortured spirits called Pretas have big stomachs and very small gullets and can neither eat nor drink, and suffer constant thirst. Therefore the allusion to " not even hearing the name of water."

The ten virtues—These are abstaining from the three evils of the body, four evils of the speech and three evils of the mind. These evils consist of: murder, theft and adultery, evils of the body; lying, slander, abusive and idle talk, evils of speech; and lust, anger and ignorance, evils of the mind. Hence the Buddhist saying, " Guard the Body, Speech and Mind! "

The three most Precious Ones—The Buddha, the doctrine and the priesthood, i.e. Buddha, Dharma and Sangha.

Kalpa—At the end of each kalpa, an incalculable number of years (4,300,000,000) the world is destroyed, each time by another means. At the end of this kalpa it will be destroyed by fire. In " The Discourse of the Seven Suns " by The Blessed One, there is a detailed description of this. Cf. Warren, *Buddhism in Translation*, pp. 321 *et seq.*

Mount Sumeru—The sacred mountain in the centre of the Buddhist Universe (a sort of Mt. Olympus). In Buddhist cosmology, Mt. Sumeru stands in the centre surrounded by oceans, mountain ranges, the various continents, planets, sun, moon and stars.

Doctrine—The " Garments of the doctrine " are the saffron yellow robes of the monks.

Arhants—Literally " Deserving Ones." Those who have " conquered the enemies ", i.e. the spiritual enemies and the desire for life and material things which lead to rebirth on the wheel of transmigration.

This parable deals with the " searchers " after knowledge. The Deity of the Ocean represents the world of Maya (Illusion). The novice by his correct answers to the questions of the deity, shows how a knowledge and practise of the basic Buddhist Doctrine leads to Right Understanding, rebirth into Superior Worlds and eventually to Arhantship, and escape from the Wheel of Transmigration.

སརྦ་མངྒ་ལཾ

Flower of the Gods

At one time these words were heard by me.

At the time the Victoriously Consummated One was dwelling in Nanyod, in the grove of King Rgyal-byed in the monastery enclosure of the Householder Who Made Food Offerings. Thousands of monks took orders and were dwelling there at the same time. In this country also there was a householder of great and noble lineage to whose wife a boy was born.

The boy was handsome and his body was of a surpassing beauty. At the moment of birth a harvest of flowers descended by magic, like rain from the heaven of the Gods, and filled the whole house. Therefore he was called Lhai Metog, " Flower of the Gods."

When the boy was grown, he went to the place where the Buddha was. Upon seeing the body colour and incomparable physical perfections of the Buddha, the youth rejoiced and thought: " Since I am born again into this world and am so blessed as to meet the noble company of Buddha and the priesthood, I would like to invite them to make food offerings." Thus he submitted to the Buddha, " It is requested that the Victoriously Consummated One, together with the noble priesthood repair to-morrow at noon to my humble abode that I might make simple food offerings." Buddha, perceiving the thought to be sincere and the purpose unselfish, accepted the invitation.

Thereafter Lhai Metog went home. The interior of the hall was magically transformed with many precious things into a residence of the Gods; it was decked with ornaments, even a throne for Buddha and seats for the priests. Various kinds of food were ready at hand for his offerings. The following day Buddha and his priests went to the house. There they were welcomed by Lhai Metog who requested them to sit down and accept the offerings. Buddha accepted the alms bowl. He then taught Lhai Metog how to increase his knowledge of the doctrine. As a result all the people of the household became faithful believers and " entered the stream."

Thereafter Lhai Metog received his parents' permission to become a disciple of the Buddha. He went to the place where Buddha stayed, put his head at the feet of the Victoriously Consummated One, and requested : " I desire the doctrine of Buddha, to become a monk."

The Buddha replied thus, " Monk, you are welcome " ; and the hair of the head of Lhai Metog and his beard fell off and his clothes became the saffron colour of the garb of the monks. Afterwards, by striving earnestly in accordance with the command of Buddha, he became an Arhant, a Conqueror of Enemies.

Thereafter, Ananda—witnessing all this—went to the place where Buddha was and, putting his knee to the earth, spoke thus : " It is requested of the Victoriously Consummated One that he tell us by virtue of what meritorious deeds performed by Lhai Metog in former lives did flowers of the Gods descend by themselves and a precious throne and various foods appear by magic." The Victoriously Consummated One explained: "Listen attentively if you desire to hear.

"In times past, when the Buddha Kanakamuni came in the world he increased the welfare of sentient beings by the teaching of the holy doctrine. Householders of high and noble lineage made gift offerings or sacrifices to the priests roving through the villages. A poor man of no possessions whatever rejoiced over the presence of the priesthood and sought for offerings. Because he had nothing whatever to bring as offerings, he gathered flowers of the woods and meadows and these, with thoughts of reverence, he strewed before the priests.

"At this time in the world, the poor man of that former period is the monk Lhai Metog. Because, in former lives, with pure and faithful thoughts he gathered flowers and strewed them before the priests like prayers, for ninety-one kalpas, whoever and wherever he is born again, he will be provided with body and form of surpassing beauty, and with meat and drink, throne cushions and wealth, unlimited. Therefore, Ananda, by all beings let it not be despised as without merit to bestow a little. Thus Lhai Metog turned towards wealth and fulfilment."

Ananda and the retinue rejoiced manifestly by hearing the explanation of Buddha.

NOTES

Buddha—One who has attained Bodhi, Enlightenment.

Body colour and perfection—The attributes of a Buddha are said to be 32 major and 80 minor marks, as for example: A Buddha has certain proportions: 40 teeth, hair curling to the right, long ears, webbed fingers, and other characteristics.

Entering the stream—The first of the Four Stages on the Path to Liberation or Nirvana. There are 4 stages on this Path: (1) Entering the stream; (2) Returning only once more to the world; (3) Never returning to this world; (4) Attaining Nirvana.

"*Hair and beard fell off*"—Symbolic of becoming a Buddhist monk with the shaven head.

Saffron colour—Monks wear saffron coloured robes.

A compensation for having made a reverent offering in a previous life, results in accumulation of merit and Good Karma. No matter how small the offering, if given with reverence and understanding, it will lead to the reward of merit.

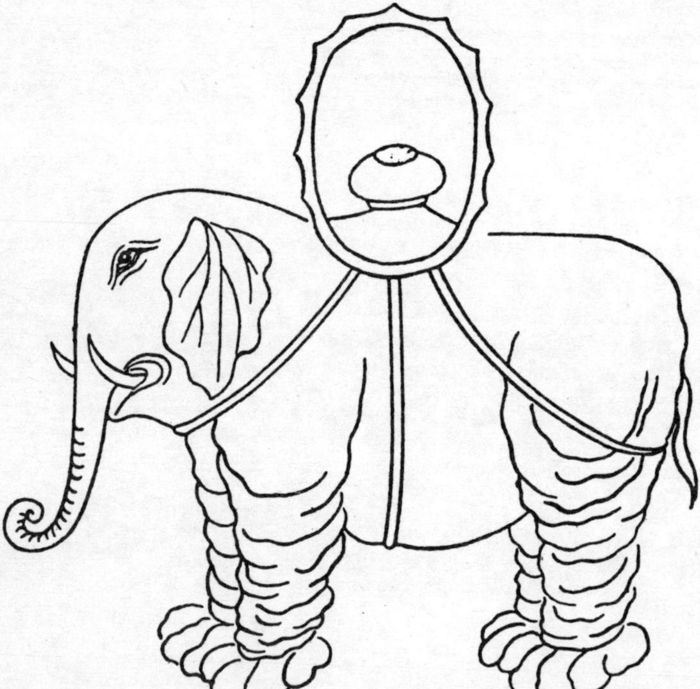

The Golden Bowls

At one time these words were heard by me.

"THE VICTORIOUSLY CONSUMMATED ONE" was dwelling at Nanyod in the grove of Prince Rgyal Byed in the enclosure of Mgon-med-zas-sbyin, the Householder who made food offerings. During the summer season many of the monks had set out on their missionary work. On returning they came together at the place where the Buddha stayed.

The Victoriously Consummated One and the monks had not met for a long time. The Buddha, remembering them with compassion and raising his hand with the wheel of a thousand spokes and treating the monks and retinue with honour, said: "When you were away, you were not ill and alms were not sparingly bestowed?" The monk Ananda, seeing Tathagata doing honour to the monks, was surprised and to the Victoriously Consummated One he submitted these words.

"The Buddha is indeed the highest excellence in the world, surely a mind beyond the reach of human intellect. Why does he condescend to do honour to the monks?" Thus he submitted and the Victoriously Consummated One said these words to Ananda, "In former kalpas innumerable, by mind inconceivable, in the place Jambudvipa, in the city of Benares, there was a householder who, by wise husbandry, transformed much wealth to gold. Making one bowl of gold, he later concealed it in the earth. In spite of his wealth, he did not get enjoyment, but changed it into gold. After a long time, the golden bowls increased to seven. He concealed all of them in the earth. Later this householder was taken ill and he died. He was reborn as a venomous serpent, coiled in a golden bowl guarding the gold.

" After a long time elapsed, the city became deserted. The serpent dying again, was reborn, in the same body, lying coiled on the golden bowls. After many ten thousand years elapsed, he was weary of being endlessly reborn in this serpent body and thought: " I myself am to blame because of attachment to this gold and must suffer this ugly body. Why do I not think of giving the gold in the field of virtue ? " (i.e. to gain merit ?) Thus thinking he concealed himself in a clump of grass to call men passing along this way.

" At this time, a man coming along the way, the venomous snake seeing him, called. The voice was heard by the man. Looking to and fro, but not seeing anyone, he entered the road and again the serpent called : ' Come near to me,' and the man said, ' For what reason do you call me ? You are a very poisonous being, you might kill me.' The serpent answered, ' Even if you do not come near me, I am still able to do harm.' The man, terrified, approached the serpent, who then said,

'By giving this golden bowl to you, will you use it toward doing good—if not, I will harm you.' The man said, 'I am willing.' He was conducted by the serpent near to the golden bowls. The serpent gave him one bowl, saying, 'This gold mass, take it away, ask the priesthood to an offering feast, I will wait near by, and then you come to meet me.' Thus he spoke.

"Thereafter the man carried the gold to the place of the community of the monks. Arriving there, he gave the gold to a monk saying, 'This gold belongs to a venomous snake who said it was to be used to make an offering feast for the priesthood.' Thereafter it was prepared and the auspicious time for the feast was calculated.

"On that day, the man carrying a basket went to the place where the venomous snake waited. The snake seeing him coming was very glad. The man put the snake in his basket and returned. On the way he met another man. This one said, 'From where do you come?' He asked him three times, but the man carrying the snake, did not answer. The snake becoming angry was about to emit poison, but thought, 'Since this man is doing a good deed for me, I must be grateful and not poison him. This man is doing a benefit for my welfare, and even if he is sinful, I must have patience.'

"Then approaching a solitary place, the serpent said to the man, 'Put me down a little,' and reproved him for not answering. He replied to the snake, 'I repentently acknowledge my sin.' Thus speaking, he carried the snake again, and came to the place where the monks were. They arrived at the time they were descending for the mid-day meal. The man distributed flowers to the priests. The snake, with devotional thought, saw the flowers scattered. Afterwards, the monks having washed their mouths and their hands after eating, explained the doctrine to the snake. The snake was very glad, and gave the other six golden bowls to the priests. Because of these good actions he soon 'changed life' and was reborn into the Heaven of the Thirty-three Gods.

"Ananda, in this life, the man who carried

the venomous snake, this man, I am. The venomous snake, indeed, is now the disciple Saribu. In that past time, while carrying the snake, I was reprimanded for my rudeness and remained humble, so now I also meet the priests with humility." Ananda and the others, hearing the explanations of the Buddha, were manifestly glad.

NOTES

Victoriously Consummated One—
Entering the Stream—
Hair and beard falling—
Saffron robe—
Arhant—

} See notes at end of " Flower of the Gods."

" *Wheel of a thousand spokes* "—The Tibetan reads, " Hand possessed of the wheel of a thousand spokes." Sometimes the Buddha is represented with the imprint of the " Wheel of the Law " on the palms of his hands.

Tathagata—A title of the Buddha derived from " tatha-agata " (thus come) and " tatha-gata " (thus gone) and giving the meaning " He who has come and gone as former Buddhas ", i.e. teaching the same truths, and following the Path to the same Goal. When Buddha preached his first sermon in the Deer Park near Benares, it was called " Turning the Wheel of the Law " and symbolised the beginning or putting in motion the Doctrine of the Buddha.

Jambhudvipa—The Buddhist Universe. Comprises Mt. Sumeru, the centre of the Universe, surrounded by oceans and mountain ranges; The four types of continents: (1) round; (2) crescent shaped; (3) square; and (4) shaped like " The shoulder blade of a sheep ," and the sun, moon and constellations. Our continent Jambhudvipa is one of those like the shoulder blade of a sheep.

" *Changed life* "—In the Tibetan language one of the expressions of " to die " is to " change life " because, except for those beings who have reached perfection and attained Nirvana, all are reborn into one of the six Regions of Rebirth: (1) the Region of the Gods; (2) The Demi-gods; (3) Man; (4) Beasts; (5) Tortured Spirits; (6) Hell.

" Calculated the auspicious time "—Before any important event is arranged it is first determined by the lama astrologer as to whether the time is auspicious or not. There are books and charts containing formulae by which the lamas decide which days are the lucky ones.

This parable deals with the results of greed. Gold when not put to good use, leads to evil and a bad rebirth.

A Son of Two Families

At one time these words were heard by me.

"THE VICTORIOUSLY CONSUMMATED ONE" was dwelling at Sravasti in the park of Prince Gyalbyed in the All-joy enclosure of Mgon-med-zas-sbyin. At that time in this country, a rich householder had a wife of equal birth, but not having a son, she was very unhappy. She made a request to the Gods. After this, she became pregnant and at the end of her pregnancy a boy was born. This boy was very handsome and very beautiful. The parents and relatives joyously made a feast. They were eating close by the river and at the time of the feast one by one they took the boy on their laps in order to see him. Being thus taken from one to the other of the family, one who was lazy or careless allowed the boy to slip away. Descending towards the water, the boy was swept away and because his destiny had not yet been fulfilled, he did not die. Swallowed by a fish, he remained preserved in the belly of the fish.

The end of this river was also in this city. In the same city, there was a rich householder who had no son. The servants of this householder were fishing near the river. Among the servants there was one who seeing the fish and grasping it,, cut open the belly, and from the belly, the boy emerged. The servant carried him away, gave him to his mistress. The wife of the householder was very glad, seeing the boy, and took him. He was possessed with good marks, and she thought: "This is because of continually requesting all the Gods." She handed him over to a nurse and brought him up as a foster son. At this time, the householder in the upper part of this city hearing that another householder in the lower part of the city had obtained a boy from the belly of a fish thought: "Certainly this boy is mine who descended into the water." Going to the other householder, he said, "This boy from the belly of the fish is surely mine, therefore give him to me." The other householder answered, "Indeed this is not your son; because I had no son, I made a request to all the Gods and they bestowed a son, who was obtained from the belly of a fish."

Thus he spoke. The two householders disputing, requested the King to make a decision. "Indeed this boy is my son, who descended into the water by the river bank," the householder said. The other householder said, "The boy is mine, I obtained him from the belly of the caught fish. He is not your son." The King said in accordance with law, "Let this boy be brought up by both together. When he is grown up, this son of both families, let each family give him a wife. Again to whichever wife a son is born, let him take that family as his." Thus he decided.

Thereafter both householders agreed to the King's decision, bringing up the boy together.

Afterwards, when the youth was grown up, he submitted this request to all his parents. "I desire to become a monk because so soon after I was begotten, I descended into the water yet did not suffer misery or evil and did not die." Thus he spoke. Though both sets of parents wondered at the beloved youth, they gave him their permission to become a monk. The youth went to the place where the Buddha was and on arriving there, he placed his head at the feet of the Buddha, and made obeisance. "I request the teaching of Buddha, in order to become a monk." The Victoriously Consummated One said to him, "You are welcome." Thus commanding, hair and beard fell out by itself. He became a monk. He also received the name "Rigsgnispa". The vows of the doctrine were explained by the Victoriously Consummated One to Rigsgnispa. He came near to the end of suffering, and turned towards becoming an Arhant.

Doubts arising among the monks, the venerable Ananda, submitted this request to the Victoriously Consummated One. "This monk, Rigsgnispa, by what root of former virtues gathered up, did he descend into the water, and exist in the belly of a fish and did not die?" The Victoriously Consummated One said to Ananda, "You listen attentively: A former Buddha, called Vipasyi came into the world and taught the doctrine to many beings. At that time, this householder also came into this circle. Hearing the teaching in great detail by the Victoriously Consummated One, of the merits of bestowing alms and of keeping the moral laws, he was very joyful and happy. Thoughts of pure faith arising, pondering on some verses of the doctrine, not to take life, and so forth, he gave to the Buddha a coin. By this merit, wherever and into whatever class of beings he will be reborn, he will possess great enjoyment and riches and will not want. Ananda, at the time of this life, the householder was indeed this monk Rigsgnispa. By giving the coin to the Buddha, he will for a period of 91 kalpas turn towards possession of great riches. In this life, also, the both pair of parents will also possess enjoyment and riches. Pondering on the verses of the doctrine not to take life, he descended into the water, remained in the belly of the fish yet did not die. Going for protection to "The Three Precious Ones," meeting with me, he became a "Conqueror of Enemies," At this time Ananda and many of the retinue rejoiced greatly at the teaching of the Victoriously Consummated One.

NOTES

The Three Precious Ones—Buddha, the Law and the Community of Priests.

Anterior Buddha—A Buddha of a past era—before Gautama, the historical Buddha.

Not to take life—The first of the 5 commandments of Buddha. This applies not only to human life but to all sentient beings.

This parable shows how Karma must be fulfilled. The son of the Householder who made an offering to the Buddha in a previous existence and learned the Doctrine from Him, was protected in this life, saved, and allowed to fulfill his destiny which was to become a disciple of the Buddha.

Gold Treasure

At one time these words were heard by me.

"THE VICTORIOUSLY CONSUMMATED ONE" was dwelling in Nanyod, in the grove of Prince Gyalbyed in the monastery of the Householder Who Made Food Offerings, in company with more than 1,250 monks.

At this time in the city, the wife of a householder gave birth to a boy, who was later called gSer dByig. The boy had a body of surpassing beauty, whose like was not to be found elsewhere in the world. Because of deeds of former lives, he was born with both hands tightly clenched. Seeing this, the parents were very astonished and when they opened his fists they found a gold coin in each. They regarded it as an omen of good luck and, therefore, named him Gold Treasure.

They were very happy and took the coins from their son's hands. The empty places were again filled with gold. Although they continued taking the coins, more always appeared. Even after the household treasury was filled, the gold in the palms of their son's hands was not exhausted.

When the boy was grown he submitted to his parents the request to take holy orders, and permission was granted. He went to the dwelling place of the Victoriously Consummated One.

At the feet of the Buddha he made obeisance and submitted this request: "It is requested of the Victoriously Consummated One himself, out of compassion to teach me, and allow me to take orders." The request was granted thus by the Victoriously Consummated One. "Youth, Gold Treasure, thou art commanded. Take thou holy orders." And Gold Treasure shaved hair and beard and donned the garb of a novice. Later, having served his novitiate, he presented himself for ordination into the priesthood. He prayed for consecration and made obeisance to each one of the priests in turn. Each time his hands touched the earth, there were gold coins. After being ordained he continued to strive diligently and became an Arhant.

Then did Ananda seek an answer of the Victoriously Consummated One, saying, "It is requested of the Victoriously Consummated One that he tell us what meritorious deeds were done in former lives, that the monk Gold Treasure, from birth even to this day, carries gold coins." The Victoriously Consummated One spoke thus: "Listen well, pay attention, and I will tell you.

"In times past, 91 kalpas ago, when the Buddha gSer-tub appeared in the world, the welfare of sentient beings was established immeasurably through Holy Doctrine. While this Buddha, accompanied by the priests, wandered from place to place, householders of noble birth and great wealth prepared many kinds of food and offerings and brought them as gifts to honour the Buddha and his company.

"A poor man of no possessions, a gatherer of wood in the hills, sold some wood of his gathering for two gold coins. Upon seeing Buddha and the monks returning from a visit to the palace of the King, he rejoiced and offered to them both coins, his only possessions.

"The Victoriously Consummated One, thinking of him with compassion, accepted the offering. Because of this sacrifice, for the period of 91 kalpas this poor one will be born with hands always holding gold coins and will live in enjoyment of wealth and riches unlimited.

"The poor man of that former period is now the monk Gold Treasure. Even though this man did not obtain the ultimate reward of becoming a Buddha, nevertheless the future rewards are immeasurable. Therefore, Ananda, should all sentient beings strive to give alms and make offerings."

Ananda and the numerous retinue, by listening and hearing the Buddha turned towards faithfully believing. A few "entered the stream"; a few, indeed, obtained the reward of coming back to earth only once more; a few of not coming back to earth again, a few becoming Arhants; and a few, indeed, who had the desire to reach the highest perfection and become Buddhas, and not come back to this earth. All listening to the Buddha rejoiced greatly.

NOTES

This parable explains the reward of sacrifice and unselfishness. The reward always fits in some way with the offering itself. Ultimately, hearing and believing the Doctrine explained by the Buddha, they " entered the stream " which is entering upon the Path to Liberation from constant Rebirth or the Wheel of Transmigration. The Four Stages of the Path are :

1. He who enters the Stream.
2. He who will return only once more to the World.
3. He who will never return to the World.
4. He who attains Arhantship.

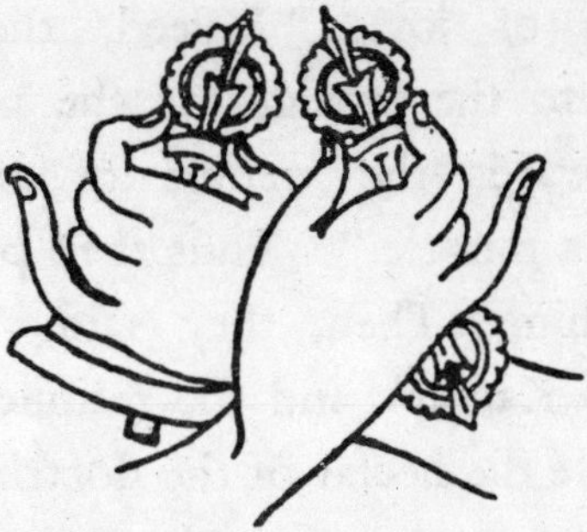

The Patient One

At one time these words were heard by me.

"THE VICTORIOUSLY CONSUMMATED ONE" was dwelling in Rajagrha in the bamboo grove, the abode of the bird Kalantaka. At this time, the Victoriously Consummated One had by complete fulfilment become the Buddha. A short time after this, the first five monks took religious orders, Kondina and four others. Afterwards, beginning with Nadi Kasyapa and his brothers, altogether one thousand monks took religious orders. From that time on, an unusual number having taken vows, many remained in the order.

The courtiers in the household of the King were full of joy. "Indeed, the Buddha coming into the world, for the purpose of acting towards the welfare of all sentient beings, is a miracle." Thus they praised and glorified him. Then, they said, "Kondina with Nadi Kasyapa and the retinue were the first to taste the nectar of the doctrine." The monks hearing these words submitted their questions in detail to the Victoriously Consummated One and he granted their requests thus. "In times long past, a great vow was made by me for your sakes, that at the time when I become the completely fulfilled Buddha, I will work towards your complete welfare." The monks hearing these words, said, "We request the Victoriously Consummated One, remembering us with compassion, to explain how the vow was made and accomplished."

The Victoriously Consummated One said to the monks, "Listen and remember, and I will show you. In times long past, kalpas immeasurable, innumerable, not to be comprehended by thoughts or by words, there lived a king, the so-called "Quarrelsome", in a place called Benares. In this country, at that time, a hermit called " The Patient One " dwelt with his retinue of five-hundred pupils, in a mountain abode. He practised forbearance. The King and his Consort and palace retinue, together with the ministers went to the hills on a pleasure trip. The King becoming tired, settled down and while sleeping, the retinue went in advance to see the woods and the flowers ; going on, they saw a hermit " The Patient One," sitting straight and of such compassionate aspect that it produced in their minds thoughts of love and faith in him. They scattered flowers of various kinds and approaching him, sat down to hear the Doctrine.

When the King awoke, not seeing the women, he went with four of his ministers to seek them. Seeing them sitting in front of the Hermit, he spoke these words, " Were the Four meditations of the endless Origin of the Senses obtained by you ? " The Hermit said, " I did not obtain them." " But did you obtain the four Immeasurables ? " " I did not obtain them." " But did you obtain the Four states of complete abstraction?" "I also did not obtain them," he replied. Then the King was angry and said, "Since these good qualities were not obtained by you, then you are certainly an ordinary person of low class. In what way is it suitable to believe one who is sitting in a lonely, solitary, protected place with women? Who are you who are always sitting here in this place? What deeds and works are you doing?"

The King having said this, the Hermit answered him, "I practice patience." Then the King, drawing out his sword, said, "If you say you practice patience, I shall see whether or not you have it." Then he cut off the two hands of the Hermit. "You, who are you?" the King asked. "I am the Patient One," the Hermit answered. Then the King cut off both feet. But still the Hermit said, "I am the Patient One." At this moment the region was shaken in six ways and as many as 500 disciples in the heavens, flying to the Teacher said to him, "Is your practice of patience not impaired by suffering such misery?" The Hermit replied,

"My thoughts are not changed and are not impaired."

The King in great fear, said to the Hermit, "Who would believe you are the Patient One?" The Hermit replied, "If my words are truth and not falsehood, by this truth may the blood turn to milk and the members which you cut off again be restored exactly as before." As he said this, the blood turned to milk and the members were restored, exactly as before. Then the King seeing endurance like this, was exceedingly fearful and full of terror. "On account of what, was the injury to this great Hermit, done by me? Remember me with compassion and grant that my repentance and remorse will purify me." The Hermit spoke, "For the sake of the women, you seized a sword and cut off my members, while I remained enduring like the earth itself. In the future when I openly become the Buddha, I will cut off your 'three poisons' by the sword of knowledge."

At this time, the hill dragons and deities seeing such injury done to the Hermit became angry and decided: each one, in his place, amassing clouds, thunder and hail and lightning, threw down thunderbolts for the purpose of killing the King and his retinue. The Hermit implored, "Because of me do not harm or injure anyone here." After this, the King having made a remorseful confession to him, invited the Hermit to the palace and made offerings. At that time, as many as one thousand wandering Brahmins, seeing the King reverencing another teacher, became envious and from an unseen place, they threw dirt and unclean things over the Hermit. "Those one thousand monks who scattered dirt over me, these are now Nadi Kasyapa and his one thousand pupils. Because at that time, I made the vow, 'When I openly become Buddha, by continued patience, may I wash off your dust and dirt through the nectar of life, and may you become wholly pure from all unclean desires. Thus I promised.'

"You monks if you desire to know who the Hermit, the Patient One of that time was, it was none other than I am now. King Quarrelsome and his four ministers are the same as Kandina and four monks. At this time, by practicing forbearance I made a vow that when I openly become the Buddha, the first act to be done is for the welfare of these, by freeing them entirely from misery." The monks hearing the explanations of Buddha rejoiced greatly.

NOTES

The Patient One—The Tibetan dictionaries translate "Bzod pa"—"The patient" or "enduring" or "forbearing." In ascetism it means "Perserverance, steadfast adherence to the 'Four Truths', constancy in adhering to the 'Path'".

Kalantaka—A bird, native of an island or province of India bordering on the Indian Ocean.

Four Meditations—There are four degrees of Dhyana or intense meditation; a religious exercise which the Buddhists engage in, in order to reach illumination and Arhantship.

Four Immeasurables — Love, compassion, suffering, indifference or apathy. In Buddhist philosophy these qualities have a special significance.

Four States of Contemplation—Complete abstraction is reached in the fourth stage of Dhyana which is called Samadhi.

Three Poisons—Lust, Anger and Ignorance.

The virtues of the Hermit and the triumph of forbearance and wisdom over cruelty and stupidity, are related here. It alludes also to the compassion of the Hermit towards the King who injured him.

This hermit, Bzod-pa, was the Buddha himself in a previous existence.

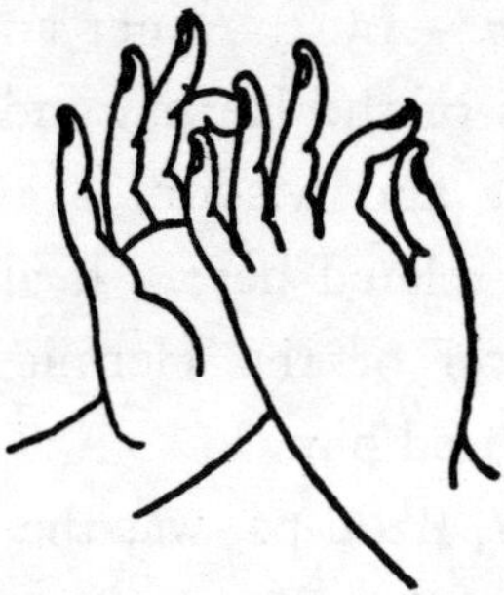

"Then the World-honoured spake: 'Scatter
not rice,
But offer loving thoughts and acts to all.
To parents as the East where rises light;
To teachers as the South whence rich gifts
come;
To wife and children as the West, where gleam
Colours of love and calm, and all days end;
To friends and kinsmen and all men as North;
To humblest living things beneath, to Saints
And Angels and the blessed Dead above:
So shall all evil be shut off, and so
The six main quarters will be safely kept.'"

The Light of Asïa,
SIR EDWIN ARNOLD.

BIBLIOGRAPHY

ARNOLD, SIR EDWIN—*The Light of Asia*, London, 1908.

BELL, SIR CHARLES—*Tibet Past and Present*, Oxford, England, 1927.

— — — *The People of Tibet*, Oxford, England, 1928.

— — — *The Religion of Tibet*, Oxford, England, 1931.

— — — *English-Tibetan Colloquial Dictionary*, Calcutta, 1920.

— — — *Grammar of Colloquial Tibetan*, Calcutta, 1919.

DAS, SARAT CHANDRA—*Tibetan-English Dictionary*, 1902.

— — — *Journey to Lhasa and Central Tibet*, London, 1902.

EVANS-WENTZ, W. Y.—*Tibetan Yoga and Secret Doctrines*, London, 1935.

GORDON, ANTOINETTE K.—*The Iconography of Tibetan Lamaism*, New York, 1939.

— — — *Tibetan Religious Art*, New York, 1952.

BIBLIOGRAPHY

JAESCHKE, H. O:—*A Tibetan-English Dictionary*, London, 1934.

KOROS, CSOMA DE—*Grammar of the Tibetan Language in English*, Calcutta, 1834.

MCGOVERN, W. M.—*A Manual of Buddhist Philosophy* (*Cosmology*), New York, 1923.

MONIER-WILLIAMS, SIR M.—*Sanskrit-English Dictionary*, Oxford, England, 1899.

ROSS, E. D.—*Mahavyutpatti—Sanskrit-Tibetan-English Dictionary*. Memoirs of the Asiatic Society of Bengal, Calcutta, 1910.

SUBHADRA, BHIKSHU—*A Buddhist Catechism*, New York, 1922.

WADDELL, L. A.—*The Buddhism of Tibet or Lamaism*, Cambridge, England, 1934.

WARREN, HENRY CLARKE—*Buddhism in Translation*, Cambridge, Massachusetts, 1947.